The Great Toilet Paper Caper

by

Gary Hogg

Illustrated by Chuck Slack

Little Buckaroo Books

For my son Boone, a boy who says he can
fly. And I believe him.

Printed August 2010 in the USA   10 9 8 7 6 5 4 3 2 1

ISBN 978-0-930771-21-8

CONTENTS

Chapter One

The World's Worst Idea

Amber's voice blared like a loudspeaker as she yelled at her younger brother. "Spencer! Move it or you'll be late for school!"

Spencer came out of his bedroom walking backwards. He tripped over a chair and crashed into the wall.

"Mom," shouted Amber. "Spencer is stuck in reverse. Do I have your permission to bonk him on the head? Maybe that will snap him out of it."

"No bonking," replied Mrs. Burton sternly. "Spencer, why on earth are you walking backwards?"

"Mom, you are looking at a boy who is going to break a world record. You can read all about it in the next edition of the *Gigantic Book of World Records*," announced Spencer.

Mrs. Burton looked worried. "Oh, son. I think this is too dangerous," she said. "All you're going to break is your leg. Isn't there a different record you would like to break?"

"Sure. I'd really like to give that knife-throwing record a try," said Spencer. "I'll need a blindfold, some sharp knives, and a dagger or two. Of course, I'll want a beautiful assistant to hold a balloon in her mouth while I throw the knives.

Maybe you could do that part, Mom."

"On second thought," replied Mrs. Burton nervously, "I think walking backwards is right up your alley."

"Thanks, Mom. Well, I better get to school. I think I'll use the *back* door." Spencer laughed.

Spencer's best friend, Josh Porter, met him at the corner.

"Hey, Spencer, you're going the wrong way," said Josh.

"No, I'm not," said Spencer, looking at his watch. "In exactly four days, six hours, and thirty-two minutes I will officially hold the world record for walking backwards."

"Wow," marveled Josh. "You're going to be famous."

"I know," said Spencer. "I can hardly wait. I've been practicing writing my autograph. I make the *S* look really wicked, like a snake with its mouth open. The rest of the letters look like the snake is spitting them out."

"I like it," said Josh, smiling. "Are you going to have blood squirting out of the snake?"

"Hey, that might be a nice touch," replied Spencer as he crashed into a tree.

"You better watch where you're going," Josh said with a laugh. "Let me be your driver for a while."

Josh took hold of Spencer's arms and began guiding him down the sidewalk. Unexpectedly, Josh reached up and twisted one of Spencer's ears.

"Hey, what was that for?" demanded Spencer.

"I was shifting gears," announced Josh as he started to walk faster.

Spencer was getting really tired as they turned into the homestretch. By the

time Josh guided him into the classroom, Spencer was completely out of gas.

Plopping down in his seat, Spencer looked around the room. It seemed that no one had noticed his backwards entrance. Even Miss Bingham hadn't looked up when Spencer backed by her desk.

Math was always the first subject of the day. Each day Miss Bingham would pick out one student to be the Math Wiz. That student would then work some problems at the chalkboard.

"The Math Wiz for today is Spencer Burton," said Miss Bingham. Spencer got up from his desk and turned around.

Miss Bingham looked very confused. "Spencer, where are you going?"

"I'm going to the chalkboard," answered Spencer, backing to the front of the room.

At first it was quiet and then a wave of laughter swept the classroom.

"Go ahead and laugh," said Spencer, banging into the chalkboard. "But I'll be the one laughing when I hold the world record for walking backwards."

"So, Spencer," said Miss Bingham, "is that what this is about? You are going to break a record? Why, that's marvelous. Now finish the problem and then back, and I mean *back*, to your seat."

Flustered at all the attention, Spencer quickly completed the math problem. He backed up the row to what he thought was his seat. Without looking, he sat down.

"Get off me, you big lug," squealed Allison. Spencer was sitting right on her lap!

He tried to get up, but Allison was pushing too hard. Spencer crashed to the floor. Everyone in the room roared with laughter.

"Are you trying to set a world record for sitting on people?" said T.J.

By the time Spencer got into his seat, he wished he could melt into it. Recess was a disaster and lunch was even worse. Everyone in the lunchroom, including the cooks, stared at Spencer like he was some kind of weirdo.

The sound of the bell to return to class was a relief. For the first time in his life Spencer wanted to sit at his desk instead of being on the playground. Spencer decided that walking backwards for four days was the worst idea he had ever come up with.

Chapter Two

Name Game

Spencer was trying to think of an excuse to explain why he couldn't break the record when Miss Bingham called the class to attention.

She was using her official voice. Miss Bingham hardly ever used her official voice. She was always having too much fun teaching to be official.

"Class, I have been thinking that we were hard on Spencer this morning. We should be more supportive of his goal."

Spencer spoke up. "That's okay, Miss Bingham, I've decided that I'm not — "

"Spencer, you don't have to say a word," Miss Bingham interrupted. "The whole class owes you an apology. And to show our support, I have decided that tomorrow will be Backwards Day for the entire class."

"But wait — " said Spencer frantically.

"There is no need to thank us, Spencer," insisted Miss Bingham. "It's the least we can do to help you in your quest for a world record."

The class began to moan. They didn't seem to be sharing Miss Bingham's enthusiasm for walking backwards.

"Relax," said Miss Bingham calmly. "It will be a fun day. We are not just going to walk backwards, we're going to do everything backwards."

"Oh, I get it," said T.J. "When we see

each other, we can say 'good-bye' for 'hello' and 'hello' for 'good-bye.' "

Becky's hand shot up. "Can we wear our clothes backwards?" she asked.

"Of course," said Miss Bingham. "And I will think up some backwards assignments for us to do."

Suddenly everyone was excited about being backwards. Miss Bingham had done it again. She had a way of taking a really horrible idea and getting everyone excited about it.

"Xer, would you please come up and help me?" asked Miss Bingham. The students looked at each other like Miss Bingham had flipped out. Who or what on earth was an Xer?

"Xer, would you please come and help me?" repeated Miss Bingham.

Suddenly a big smile popped onto Rex's face. He jumped up and marched to the front of the room.

Miss Bingham started to laugh. "I knew you would get it sooner or later."

"Get what?" asked Josh.

"Rex, would you please explain to the rest of the class?" asked Miss Bingham.

"Xer is my name spelled backwards," announced Rex.

"That's it," said Miss Bingham. "Tomorrow all of our names will be backwards. I think we better make some name tags so that we will know what to call each other."

She gave Rex a stack of colored paper. He passed out the paper while the students got out their markers.

"Let's be creative," advised Miss Bingham. "Decorate your name tags any way you want. Just be sure that your name is spelled backwards."

Soon every member of the class had his or her imagination cooking. Spencer thought this would be a good time to use

his snake idea. He turned the *S* in his name into a mean-looking green snake.

Josh looked at Spencer's name tag and started to laugh. "Hey, Recneps, nice snake."

Spencer started to laugh too. "Thanks Hsoj," he said.

"This isn't fair," called out T.J. "My name spelled backwards is J.T. That's not very fun."

"What does the *T* and *J* stand for?" asked Miss Bingham.

"Thomas James," replied T.J.

"Then you are Semaj Samoht," announced Miss Bingham.

"Awesome!" said T.J. excitedly as he went back to work on his name tag.

Soon the air was filled with laughter and names like Ykceb, Nosilla, Neb, and Irol.

Chapter Three

Backwards Day

The next morning, the students were all laughing as they backed into their seats. Rex kept trying to talk backwards, but no one could tell what he was saying.

When the bell rang, Miss Bingham came walking through the door backwards. Her glasses were on the back of her head.

"Good-bye, class," she said as she faced the chalkboard.

"Good-bye, Miss Bingham," the class called out.

"Last thing this afternoon," she announced, which meant first thing this morning, "we will have a test."

The students mumbled complaints as Miss Bingham handed out the test.

"I thought Backwards Day was going to be fun," moaned T.J.

"Hey, what's going on?" asked Becky. "These aren't questions. They're answers."

"That's right," said Miss Bingham. "This is a backwards test. It is your job to write the questions."

Soon the children in the class were laughing as they wrote silly questions to fit the answers.

Suddenly the door opened and Mr. Warner, the principal, came into the room.

"Miss Bingham told me about Backwards Day, so I thought I'd have a look for myself. Spencer, I hear that you started this whole thing. Miss Bingham said you are trying to set a world record. I think that's just great."

Becky raised her hand. "Mr. Warner, do you hold any world records?"

"I'm afraid not." He paused for a minute. "But if I did, I would be very, very proud."

"What about your ears?" blurted out Josh. "They're pretty big. You should measure them. They might be a record."

"Joshua!" snapped an embarrassed Miss Bingham.

"Sorry, Josh," said Mr. Warner. "I know they are bigger than a lot of people's, but they are no world record."

"Don't feel bad," said Allison. "You hold the record for being the best principal at our school." She thought for a second and added, "Of course, you are the

only principal at our school. But if there were a whole bunch, you would still be the best."

Mr. Warner laughed. "Thank you, Allison. I guess it's just not in the cards for me to be famous. Well, I better go so you can get *back* to work."

"Thank you for coming, Mr. Ears — I mean, Mr. Warner," said Miss Bingham. The class laughed and Miss Bingham's face turned bright red. "I'm sorry," she quickly added.

Backwards Day was a blast. Everything the class did was fun. Miss Bingham had plenty of backwards things for them to do.

The whole class played backwards musical chairs. Miss Bingham even had the students line up and dance the Backwards Bunny Hop.

At recess, the class played backwards kickball. A big crowd gathered to cheer the players on. Soon the entire school was talking about Miss Bingham's backwards class.

Spencer enjoyed the day too, but he was glad it was almost over. He still didn't like walking backwards. He only hoped that tomorrow everyone would have forgotten about his crazy idea.

"May I have your attention, please?" Mr. Warner's voice came over the intercom. "It's time to announce the class of the day award. Today's honor goes to a class that loves my ears.

"Miss Bingham and her class have shown us that laughing and learning can go hand in hand. They win the award."

Spencer's class erupted into applause.

Mr. Warner continued, "After seeing the fun that this class has had today, I have received many requests for a school Backwards Day. After discussing it with the teachers, I have decided that this Friday will be Crestview Elementary School Backwards Day. The monthly awards assembly will cap off our day of backwards activities.

"I should say that this all came about because of Spencer Burton. He's trying to set a record for walking backwards. When you see him, be sure to give him some encouragement."

That sealed it. There was no turning back now. Spencer had no choice. He had to spend the next three days of his life in reverse.

Chapter Four

Operation T.P.

"**M**r. Warner sure gives out a lot of awards," said Josh as the students in Miss Bingham's class began preparing for the final bell.

"Yeah, he's a really nice guy," added Allison. "Somebody should give him an award."

"That is an excellent idea," said Miss Bingham. "We could present him with an award at the assembly this Friday."

"Awards are nice," said Spencer. "But being famous is a lot better. Why don't we give him a world record? That way we would be giving him more than a certificate. We would be making him famous."

"You heard him this morning," responded Rex. "His ears are big, but they're no world record."

Spencer pulled the *Gigantic Book of World Records* out of his desk. "In this book, there are thousands of different kinds of world records. I'm sure that we can find one for Mr. Warner."

"I like your idea," Miss Bingham said. "But whatever we decide to do must be something in which we can all participate."

Josh's arm shot up. "We could make him the world's biggest banana split. Then we could help him eat it."

Spencer quickly looked the record up in the book. "The current record for a banana split was made with over forty-five thousand gallons of ice cream."

Rex always had his calculator ready. He punched in the numbers and announced, "That means we would each have to bring in one thousand nine hundred and fifty-six gallons of ice cream." Making the world's biggest banana split was out of the question.

"We could give him the world's smelliest socks. They're my dad's, but I think we can borrow them," said Alex.

"I think we'll pass on that one," said Miss Bingham, wrinkling her nose.

"Mr. Warner always wears ties," said Allison.

"That's it," said Josh. "My mom says that Mr. Warner has the ugliest ties. I'll bet one of them is the world's ugliest."

"Josh," moaned Allison. "I was thinking that we could make him the world's longest tie."

Spencer flipped through the pages of the book. "The world's longest tie is two miles long," he announced.

"If we build one hundred feet of tie a day, it would take us a hundred and five point six days," chimed in Rex, his fingers flying over his calculator.

"Hey, wait a minute," Spencer called out. "Right under ties there is a record that we have a good shot at breaking. The world's largest roll of toilet paper is only six feet four and a half inches tall."

Spencer stood up and looked around the classroom. "We could build one bigger than that. And I'll bet that almost everyone in this room has some toilet paper at home."

Some of the kids started to moan. Miss Bingham spoke up. "Now, wait, class. Spencer might have something here. It's a little unusual, but he's right. We can all get our hands on toilet paper. All in favor of building a record roll of toilet paper, raise your hand."

Everyone but T.J. raised a hand. He was still dreaming about the world's largest banana split.

"That settles it," said Miss Bingham. "The assembly is this Friday, so let's start collecting paper right away. This is going to be a surprise, so let's keep it as quiet as possible."

"We need a code name for this mission!" exclaimed Josh.

"How about Operation T.P.?" responded Rex.

Soon everyone was chanting, "T.P., T.P."

The excitement was interrupted by the bell. The students quickly put their books away and headed out the door.

"Wait up," Spencer called to Josh. "You're in second gear and I'm stuck in reverse."

Chapter Five

Toilet Paper Tightwad

"How was school?" asked Mrs. Burton as Spencer backed through the front door. She was busy dusting the furniture.

"It was fun. All of the other classes were jealous. So this Friday, the whole school is having a Backwards Day."

"Spencer, that sounds wonderful," Mrs. Burton said. "It looks like you've started something that's really catching on."

"Oh, yeah," added Spencer, "I almost forgot the best part. Our class is going to give Mr. Warner a world record."

"What kind of world record can you give somebody?" asked Mrs. Burton.

"We're going to make him the world's largest — " Suddenly Spencer stopped. "Mom, you can't tell anyone. We have to keep it a secret."

"Your secret's safe with me," Mrs. Burton promised, crossing her heart.

"We are going to make the world's biggest roll of toilet paper," Spencer proudly announced.

Spencer's mother burst out laughing. "You've got to be kidding."

"It's going to be great," said Spencer excitedly. "Everyone in the class has to bring some rolls from home. How many rolls can we spare? Fifty or sixty?"

"Oh, not that many," said Mrs. Burton. "Perhaps we can give three or four."

"Is that all?" whined Spencer. "Mom, you don't understand, we need a ton of T.P. Our roll has to be over six feet tall."

"I'm sorry, son, that's all you're going to get." Mrs. Burton finished dusting the top of the piano and headed for the kitchen.

Spencer backed to his bedroom and flopped onto his bed. His hopes of bringing in more toilet paper than anyone else were suddenly dashed.

How could he face the class with just four rolls? He had to get more. Much, much more. That's when Spencer remembered something his neighbor, Mr. Hiskey, once told him.

"Spencer, my boy, it is the duty of every red-blooded American to have enough basic supplies on hand to last at least two years."

That advice had caused Spencer a lot

of trouble. He had spent a whole week trying to convince his parents that he needed to have a two-year supply of candy on hand at all times.

If Mr. Hiskey had enough toilet paper to last for two years, he should have plenty to share.

Spencer grabbed his backpack and backed out. Soon he was standing on the Hiskeys' front porch.

Spencer was about to ring the doorbell when he spotted the video camera. Mr. Hiskey had mounted a camera above his door as a security measure. He wasn't going to let anyone in his house without first checking that person out.

Spencer had never met a camera he didn't like. All of a sudden, it was "The Spencer Burton Show," live, from Mr. Hiskey's porch.

He started off with some of his basic

funny faces. He stuck out his tongue, and made moose antlers with his hands.

Spencer then moved on to some more advanced faces such as the disgusting pig-nose boy. He was just getting into his specialty, a crossed-eye, double-nostril flare with a tongue flap, when the door flew open.

Mr. Hiskey dashed out of the open door. "Stop that," he shouted. "Are you trying to make us sick? We are trying to have our dinner in there."

"Oh, I'm sorry," said Spencer, trying to keep from smiling. It was nice to know that all of that practice at making faces was finally paying off.

"Mr. Hiskey, I'm collecting toilet paper. Do you have some you could spare?"

Spencer knew this was a silly question. Mr. Hiskey had about a thousand rolls of toilet paper in his emergency supply room.

Mr. Hiskey closed one eye and stared at Spencer. "Toilet paper," he muttered to himself. "The neighbor boy wants some toilet paper."

"It's for a school project," added Spencer.

"You young people of today take things like toilet paper for granted. Why, in my day we treated toilet paper with respect. We were grateful for every little piece. Toilet paper was our friend."

Spencer wasn't interested in having toilet paper for a friend. Disappointed, Spencer started to back off the porch, but Mr. Hiskey stopped him.

"Where are you going?" demanded Mr. Hiskey. "You're not leaving without some toilet paper. No one can say that Horace Hiskey doesn't support the local school. How much do you want?"

"Well . . ." said Spencer. He was trying to think of the right number.

He was about to answer when Mr. Hiskey spoke up. "How about a dozen?"

"Wow, a dozen would be just perfect," said Spencer excitedly.

He was opening his backpack to prepare for the big load when Mr. Hiskey returned.

"There you go," he said, "twelve squares of toilet paper." Mr. Hiskey handed Spencer a small pile of carefully folded toilet paper. "I left them connected together."

"But Mr. Hiskey — "

"There's no need to thank me. All I ask is that you treat them with respect," said Mr. Hiskey as he closed the door.

Spencer couldn't believe it. Mr. Hiskey, who had more toilet paper than anyone

else in town, only gave up twelve lousy squares.

"What a toilet paper tightwad," muttered Spencer. "I hope everybody else isn't so stingy with their toilet paper." He shoved the tissue into his pack and backed on down the street.

Chapter Six

Secret Agent Jake

Spencer was backing toward the Petersens' house when his mother pulled up alongside him. She had Amber and Spencer's little brother, Jake, in the car with her.

"Spencer, I have been looking all over for you. What are you doing?" she asked.

"I'm collecting toilet paper," Spencer replied proudly. "It's almost as fun as trick-or-treating."

"Oh, please, tell me you're not going door to door asking for toilet paper," pleaded Mrs. Burton.

"Of course I am," said Spencer. "And I'm just getting warmed up."

"Spencer Burton, get in this car right now!" demanded Mrs. Burton. "I will not have you begging for toilet paper. We'll be the talk of the neighborhood."

"We already are," said Amber. "Backwards Boy here has everyone thinking we're from Planet Goofball."

"Amber, you are not helping matters," said Mrs. Burton, pulling away from the curb. "We're going to Reggie Burgers for dinner. I hope you're all hungry."

They didn't have to wait long for their order. Reggie Burgers was known for its fast service.

Spencer backed around the restaurant looking for an empty booth. Everyone stopped eating and stared at him. He quickly sat down.

The Burtons were munching their hamburgers when Jake's eyes grew big and he shouted, "*Potty!*"

Jake was in the middle of being potty trained. Whenever he made a potty announcement, the Burtons had to react fast or suffer the wet consequences.

"Spencer, quick, take your brother to the rest room," said Mrs. Burton.

The boys rushed into the men's room. While he waited, Spencer leaned against the wall and stared at the toilet paper dispenser. It held the biggest roll of toilet paper that he had ever seen.

Spencer stared at the bright, white paper. It put him in some kind of weird toilet paper trance.

Then Spencer had an idea. It didn't seem like a crime at the time. After all, it was a rest room for the public, and he was part of the public.

Spencer grabbed hold of the paper and gave a jerk. The toilet paper rolled out of the dispenser like an avalanche. Spencer pulled again and again. The mountain of toilet paper on the floor grew and grew.

"Listen, Jake, you're going to help me sneak this toilet paper out of here," whispered Spencer in his secret agent voice. "You can be Agent 002. Your code name is Terminator."

Spencer started pushing toilet paper into Jake's shirt. Soon Jake looked like a linebacker for the Dallas Cowboys.

Then Spencer began filling his own shirt. What wouldn't fit in his shirt, he shoved into his pants.

Spencer and Jake looked like walking pillows with heads. Spencer shoved the last piece of toilet paper in his pocket

and picked up Jake. He waddled backwards out of the rest room.

The two walking pillows went back to
the booth and sat down. Mrs. Burton and
Amber stared at the chubby pair.

"Can I have some more fries?" asked
Spencer.

"It looks like you've had plenty of fries
already," said Amber. "You're as big as a
house."

"What on earth were you boys doing
in there?" asked Mrs. Burton. "You were
in there for the longest time. And then
you come out looking like . . ."

She stopped talking when she noticed
Jake tugging at a piece of toilet paper
that was sticking out from his shirt.
Spencer reached across the table to stop
him, but it was too late.

"Spencer Burton!" said Mrs. Burton.
"Don't tell me you are having your little
brother help you steal toilet paper."

"No, well, I didn't actually — " stammered Spencer.

His mother stopped him. "Well, you are going to give it right back, young man."

The jig was up. Jake had turned out to be the worst secret agent in the universe. Slowly, Spencer unstuffed himself. He cleaned out his shirt and pulled all the toilet paper out of his pants.

Mrs. Burton gathered all the paper in her arms and marched Spencer up to the front counter.

She piled the toilet paper on the counter and waited. Soon the redheaded teenager who was working at the counter came over.

"May I take your order?" he asked cheerfully.

"Toilet paper," snapped Mrs. Burton.

"Toilet paper," the young man repeated slowly. "I'm sorry, ma'am, we don't sell toilet paper. At least, I don't think we do. I'm kind of new."

He looked around and stared at the menu behind him.

"I don't want to buy toilet paper. I *have* toilet paper," Mrs. Burton announced.

"Whoa, you really do," said the boy, looking at the pile on the counter. "That's an awesome stack of T.P. What are you going to do with it?"

"I'm giving it to you," she said sternly.

"Hey," he said backing away from the counter. "If you're thinking of trading it for a burger, you can't. My boss said we can't take anything but money for the food."

"You don't understand," Mrs. Burton said sharpy. "It already belongs to you."

The young man looked at the toilet paper and then at Mrs. Burton. "It doesn't look familiar," he said, trying to make sense of this strange conversation.

Suddenly the manager came out from the back of the restaurant.

"What's the problem?" she asked.

"My son took this toilet paper from your rest room," said Mrs. Burton firmly. "We are returning it."

"Why?" asked the confused young lady.

"Because it doesn't belong to him," insisted Mrs. Burton.

"What do you want me to do with it?" asked the manager. She was becoming irritated with the Burtons and their pile of toilet paper.

"How should I know?" said Mrs. Burton.

The Burtons left while the two workers stared blankly at the giant pile of toilet paper.

Chapter Seven

The Easy Way

Spencer backed into his bedroom and closed the door. His toilet paper collection was only up to four rolls and twelve squares. He had to do better than that.

Suddenly Spencer started to smile. A great idea had just hatched in his brain.

Spencer stood up on his bed and pulled his poster of the Chicago Bulls off the wall. "Sorry, guys, but you're out of here."

Grabbing the markers out of his desk, Spencer went to work. In giant letters on the back of the poster he wrote, I NEED TOILET PAPER.

Spencer put the sign under his arm. He backed into the kitchen and picked up the phone.

When Josh answered the phone, Spencer quickly asked, "How much toilet paper have you collected?"

"My mom thinks Operation T.P. is a goofy idea. She would only give me one roll," moaned Josh.

"My mom isn't much better," complained Spencer, "but I have a plan. We'll be rolling in toilet paper in no time."

"What do you need me to do?" asked Josh eagerly.

"Jump on your bike and get over here as fast as you can."

"I'm on my way," replied Josh.

When Josh zoomed into the Burtons'

driveway, Spencer was sitting in his old red wagon, waiting. Spencer grabbed a rope out of the wagon. He quickly tied one end to the wagon and the other end to Josh's bike.

Jumping into the wagon, Spencer shouted, "To the corner of Fifth and Main, and step on it."

"You better hold on!" exclaimed Josh.

Josh pedaled his bike as fast as he could. Spencer held on for dear life as the wagon bounced over bumps and skidded around corners.

It wasn't long until they were in front of Clark's Department Store. Josh hit the brakes and slid to a stop. The red wagon crashed into the bike, sending Spencer flying onto the ground.

"Wow, what a ride," shouted Spencer as he dusted himself off.

"What do we do now?" asked Josh.

"Now we get toilet paper the easy

way," replied a confident Spencer. He unrolled the sign and held it up high.

As people passed by, they seemed very interested in Spencer's toilet paper sign. Some started to laugh, but most people looked confused and hurried by.

Spencer and Josh were starting to get discouraged when they heard the sound of squealing brakes. Mr. Burton's car came to a screeching stop. Spencer's dad jumped out and marched over to the two boys.

"What on earth are you doing?" he demanded, grabbing the sign from Spencer. Mr. Burton stood there holding the I NEED TOILET PAPER sign while Spencer tried to explain.

Spencer was just getting started when a man came by and handed Mr. Burton ten dollars.

"I hope this helps," he said, patting Mr. Burton kindly on the back.

"Wait, you — you don't understand,"

stammered Spencer's dad as the man walked away. "I don't want your money."

Mr. Burton's face glowed red. He wadded up the poster and ordered Spencer into the car.

Josh was already gone. He had jumped on his bike and kicked it into hyperspeed.

When they got home, Mrs. Burton was talking on the phone. "That is so nice, but really, it is not necessary. We are fine. We don't need any help."

She hung up the phone. "That phone has been ringing off the hook. For some strange reason, everyone in town suddenly thinks we're in the poorhouse. You didn't lose your job, did you?" she said to Mr. Burton.

"No, but I know someone who may be getting a few extra jobs around the house," said Mr. Burton as he flattened Spencer's sign out on the kitchen table.

Mrs. Burton read it and started to laugh. "Spencer, these toilet paper capers have got to stop."

"What other toilet paper capers have you had?" asked Mr. Burton.

Spencer and his mom told Mr. Burton about the events of the day. Spencer's father listened to the whole story. When they were done he shook his head. "And that cheapskate Hiskey only gave you twelve squares of toilet paper."

He pulled out the ten-dollar bill that the man had given him and handed it to Spencer. "I guess this belongs to you."

"Wow," said Spencer. "How many rolls of toilet paper do you think this will buy?"

"Enough to keep you out of trouble for a while, I hope," replied Mr. Burton.

"We are going to beat that record for sure!" shouted Spencer.

Chapter Eight

The Big Day

Backwards Day had everyone laughing. The entire school was in a good mood. But no one was having a better time than Mr. Warner.

He was wearing his suit and tie backwards. As he backed down the hall, it was hard to tell if he was coming or going. He was proudly wearing a name tag that said MR. RENRAW.

At first the halls were one giant traffic

jam. Everyone kept backing into each other. By lunchtime, things were going smoothly.

Recess was a riot. Some students were playing backwards tag. Others were riding the teeter-totters backwards. Some fifth-graders even got a hilarious game of backwards football going.

The school cooks got into the spirit of the day too. They served the potatoes on top of the gravy and upside-down cake for dessert.

The excitement was really bubbling in Spencer's class. Miss Bingham had called the offices of the *Gigantic Book of World Records*. They were sending a man named Tom Meyers to take pictures and do the paperwork.

Mr. Meyers promised to be at the school when the awards assembly began. By the time school was out, Spencer and Mr. Warner would both be famous.

All of the desks were covered with rolls of toilet paper. Every color and kind of toilet paper had been collected. Miss Bingham looked around the room and started to clap.

"You all did so well," she said, beaming. "Operation T.P. is going to be a smashing success. We have to get to work. The assembly is scheduled to begin at two o'clock. So let's get rolling."

The desks were quickly pushed back to make room for the work. Everyone in the class was assigned a job. Some were package openers. Others would loosen the first square of each roll.

Josh and T.J. were in charge of pushing the growing roll along the floor. It was like a snowball getting bigger and bigger as it rolled along.

As he pushed, T.J. made train sounds and announced, "Here comes the toilet paper express."

It wasn't long until Allison and Becky were needed to help keep the roll moving. Finally the last piece of toilet paper was attached and glued down.

The students and Miss Bingham stood back and admired the giant roll of toilet paper.

"It is beautiful!" gasped Allison. The mixture of all of the different colors of toilet paper made a colorful wheel.

"It sure is," said Miss Bingham. "Now let's see if it's big enough."

She took out a tape measure and climbed onto a chair next to the toilet paper. Miss Bingham pulled the tape measure up the side of the giant roll. The children held their breath as she took it to the very top.

Miss Bingham squinted as she looked at the numbers on the tape. "I can't believe it. This roll of toilet paper is six feet four and three-quarters inches. *We did it!*"

The classroom exploded in applause. Students began giving each other high fives and squealing with delight.

Miss Bingham gave Josh a hall pass and asked him to go and get Mr. Bench, the custodian.

The students were still celebrating when Josh and the custodian walked in. Mr. Bench took one look at the gigantic roll of toilet paper and his mouth dropped open.

He gasped. "What is that?"

"That is a world record!" replied Miss Bingham. "We are presenting it to Mr. Warner at the assembly today. Do you think you could help us roll it out?"

"Miss Bingham, it would be an honor," replied Mr. Bench. "I can't wait to see the look on Mr. Warner's face."

Mr. Bench left and the class put the

finishing touches on the picture they were creating for the occasion. It was a drawing of Mr. Warner next to the world record roll.

Josh drew the ears on Mr. Warner. Miss Bingham suggested he try not to make them look too big.

At last everything was ready. Miss Bingham was beaming. "Class, this is a wonderful project. I think we should all thank Spencer for giving us the idea."

"Three cheers for Spencer Burton," called out Josh. The entire class yelled, "Hip hip hooray! Hip hip hooray! Hip hip hooray!"

Spencer grinned from ear to ear. He could tell that being famous was really going to agree with him.

Chapter Nine

Fame and Misfortune

Crestview Elementary sat on a hill overlooking the town. It had a nice grassy courtyard where assemblies were held when the weather was nice. And today was a beautiful day.

Miss Bingham was very nervous. Tom Meyers, from the *Gigantic Book of World Records*, had not shown up yet. She kept glancing over to the parking lot.

The assembly was about to begin

when Mr. Meyers finally arrived. He was carrying a briefcase and had a camera hanging around his neck. Miss Bingham waved at him and he hurried over.

"I'm sorry I'm late," he whispered. "The world's longest snake wrapped itself around my leg and wouldn't let me go."

"Oh, dear," said Miss Bingham.

Tom Meyers started to laugh. "I'm just kidding. I had car trouble. I hope I haven't kept you waiting."

The assembly began exactly like every other assembly at Crestview. Mrs. Pullman, the music teacher, led the staff and students in singing the school song.

Then Mr. Warner stood up and walked backwards to the front of the group. Speaking into the microphone, he began, "Backwards Day has been a tremendous success. I haven't heard so much laughter in the halls since we had Crazy Hair Day. Usually we present the student and class awards at the end of the assembly. But since this is Backwards Day, we will give them out first."

Just then Mr. Bench came around the corner. He was pushing the giant roll of toilet paper. He rolled it right up to the astonished Mr. Warner.

Many of the students and teachers started to laugh. Mr. Warner just stood there, scratching his head.

Mr. Bench pointed over to Miss Bingham. "She'll explain it to you," he said.

Miss Bingham hurried to the front. She cleared her throat and began to speak. "Mr. Warner, every month we have awards assemblies. We really appreciate the awards and prizes that you hand out. My class decided that since it is Backwards Day, they would give *you* an award."

"A lifetime supply of toilet paper. How nice," said Mr. Warner.

Miss Bingham laughed. "No, that's not it. The class had a vote and decided that the best thing we could give you was a little bit of fame. Mr. Warner, this is the largest roll of toilet paper in the world. And this certificate says that it's yours. You are the owner of a world-record-breaking roll of toilet paper."

She motioned to Tom Meyers and he came to the front. "This is Mr. Tom Meyers from the *Gigantic Book of World Records*. He is going to take your picture with the roll of toilet paper. Your name and picture will be in the next edition of the *Gigantic Book of World Records*."

Mr. Warner just stood there for a minute. He was letting all of this strange news sink in. Then he started to smile — a smile so big that it might have been a world record.

"Well, this is the nicest thing anyone has ever done for me," said Mr. Warner. "I never dreamed that someday I would be the owner of a world record."

"If you'll stand next to it, I'll take the picture," said Tom Meyers.

"Wait," said Mr. Warner. "I want everyone from Miss Bingham's class in the picture, too."

Miss Bingham motioned to her class and they all came up.

"Since Spencer inspired all of this, I want him to stand right next to me," said Mr. Warner.

Spencer was so excited that he forgot to look where he was going. He backed around Josh and Allison and bumped right into the world record roll.

The gigantic roll rocked back and forth. Before anyone realized what was happening, the toilet paper began to move. It started to roll down the hill. It was bouncing higher and higher and gaining speed.

Mr. Warner took off like a shot. He was going to stop that runaway roll of toilet paper. Everyone was amazed at how fast Mr. Warner could move.

He ran past the roll and veered into its path. Spreading his legs, he braced for the crash.

The toilet paper knocked Mr. Warner down and rolled over him like he was a human bowling pin.

The teachers and students couldn't believe their eyes. The principal of Crestview Elementary had just been flattened by a giant roll of toilet paper.

Suddenly Mr. Warner sat up. "That thing is going to kill someone!" he screamed. "I've got to warn the town."

Mr. Warner ran over and jumped into his car. Turning on his emegency flashers, he raced off.

"I'm going after it," said Spencer, heading for the bike rack.

"Wait!" shouted Rex. "If you walk frontwards, you'll miss breaking the record by six minutes."

"I don't care," yelled Spencer as he grabbed the first bike he saw. "I've got to help Mr. Warner."

Spencer pushed the pedals hard as he headed for the shortcut. One way or another, he was going to stop this runaway roll of toilet paper.

Chapter Ten

Attack of the Killer Toilet Paper

The world's record roll of toilet paper sped down Sixth Street. Mr. Warner thought his only chance was to beat the toilet paper to town. He raced up the road, breaking all speed limits. His wheels screeched as he turned onto Maple Street.

Suddenly he saw flashing lights in his mirror. Sheriff Rowlan was hot on his trail. Mr. Warner quickly pulled over.

"I don't have time for this," he shouted. "A giant roll of toilet paper is headed for town. There's no telling how many people it will kill."

Sheriff Rowlan got out of the patrol car and walked slowly toward Mr. Warner. He rubbed his eyes when he saw that Mr. Warner was wearing his clothes backwards.

"Don't you understand? There is a killer roll of toilet paper on the loose," screamed Mr. Warner.

"I was afraid this would happen someday," said the sheriff. "Those kids have finally driven you nuts."

Mr. Warner threw his hands in the air. "Would you listen to me? We have got to save the town."

"I think you had better come down to the station with me," said the sheriff.

At that instant, the giant roll of toilet paper came crashing through a weed patch and onto the road. It rolled over the sheriff's foot and kept going.

Sheriff Rowlan grabbed his foot and yelled, "What on earth was that?"

"That was the killer roll of toilet paper I've been trying to tell you about," hollered Mr. Warner.

Sheriff Rowlan hopped over to his car and grabbed his police radio. "This is Sheriff Rowlan. We have an emergency. There is a giant roll of toilet paper racing through town. It is to be considered extremely dangerous."

"Excuse me," came back the reply. "Did you say toilet paper?"

"Jump in, Mr. Warner," shouted the sheriff. "We have got to stop this thing."

By the time the men were in the car, the toilet paper had rolled out of sight.

Spencer's shortcut ended in the back of Josh's yard. He came busting out of the yard at full speed. When Spencer got onto

Elm Street, he spotted the giant roll. It was headed for Reggie Burgers.

Spencer pedaled hard and was closing in on the runaway toilet paper when it hit the curb in front of the restaurant.

It bounced high in the air and zoomed past the front window just as a man was placing an order.

"I'll have a medium root beer, a Reggie Burger, and a large order of . . . *toilet paper!*" he shrieked as he looked out of the window.

"Oh, no, here we go again," said the redheaded teenager behind the counter.

Sheriff Rowlan and Mr. Warner were speeding toward the center of town. Suddenly Deputy Pickett's voice came over the radio. "Sheriff, we have received a sighting of your toilet paper. It's rolling toward the city park."

"I'm on my way," snapped the sheriff.

Sheriff Rowlan turned right onto Main

Street and floored his patrol car. He was at the park in no time. Screeching to a halt, he grabbed the loudspeaker.

"Now listen up. This is Sheriff Rowlan speaking. We have a roll of killer toilet paper headed straight for this park. We must clear the area immediately."

The park was crowded. The ladies from the Daffodils Flower Club were holding a big meeting. Mrs. Dawson marched right up to the sheriff.

"Sheriff Rowlan, I demand to know what's going on here."

"Don't you understand?" shouted the sheriff. "A giant roll of toilet paper has gone crazy. It's headed for this park!"

The runaway toilet paper roll was beginning to look tattered. The end of the paper was ragged and flapping as the roll spun around.

Spencer saw this as his chance. He gave the bike his last bit of energy and pedaled alongside the tattered roll.

Grabbing the end of the paper, Spencer hit the brakes hard. He slid to a stop, still gripping the end of the toilet paper in his hand.

Spencer held tight as the paper sped on. The giant roll was getting smaller and smaller. Like the tail of a comet, it was leaving a trail of color behind.

The sheriff had everyone in the park safely behind a barricade. They were prepared for the attack of the killer toilet paper.

As the paper got closer and closer to the park, it also got smaller and smaller. By the time it reached the barricade, it was the size of a normal roll of toilet paper. It rolled slowly up to the picnic table and stopped.

Mrs. Dawson reached down and picked it up. "Is this what you are so afraid of?" she asked.

"Well, uh . . . it seemed a lot bigger

when I saw it earlier," he stammered.

Everyone in the crowd was laughing.

"Thanks, Sheriff. Boy, you really saved us today," a man called out.

"Yeah, Sheriff," someone else yelled, "without this barricade some innocent bug or spider may have been hurt."

"Okay, you've had your fun. Now break it up," said the red-faced sheriff.

Spencer came coasting into the park on the bike. He didn't have any trouble tracking down the roll. He just followed the trail of toilet paper it left behind.

He rode over to Mr. Warner. "I'm sorry," he said. "I guess neither one of us will get a world record today."

"That's the way the toilet paper unrolls," Mr. Warner said, and laughed.

Just then, Tom Meyers drove up the road and stopped at the park. He hopped out of his car and marched over to Spencer and Mr. Warner.

"I've been looking all over for you two," he said. "Is it true that the entire student body of Crestview Elementary walked backwards all day today?"

"Yes," said Mr. Warner. "It was a lot of fun."

"It was more than just fun," said Tom Meyers, smiling. "It was a world's record."

"You've got to be kidding," said Mr. Warner, looking excited again.

"I'm totally serious," said Mr. Meyers. "Miss Bingham said the whole thing came about because of you two. Your names and pictures are going into the next edition of the *Gigantic Book of World Records.*

"If you'll move next to that tree, I'll take your picture," said Mr. Meyers.

"Yes! I knew we'd be famous!" shouted Spencer. He gave Mr. Warner a big high five and smiled the world's largest grin.